THE ELEPHANT'S CHILD

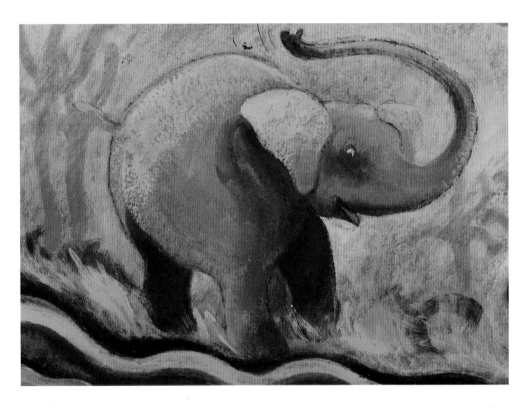

Abridged from Rudyard Kipling's *Just So Stories*
Illustrated by Geoffrey Patterson

F
FRANCES LINCOLN
CHILDREN'S BOOKS

IN THE HIGH AND FAR-OFF TIMES the Elephant, O Best Beloved, had no trunk. He only had a blackish, bulgy nose, as big as a boot, that he could wriggle about from side to side; but he couldn't pick up things with it.

But there was one Elephant — a new Elephant — an Elephant's Child — who was full of 'satiable curiosity, and that means he asked ever so many questions.

AND HE FILLED ALL AFRICA with his 'satiable curiosities. He asked his tall aunt, the Ostrich, why her tail-feathers grew just so, and his tall aunt spanked him with her hard, hard claw.

He asked his tall uncle, the Giraffe, what made his skin spotty, and his tall uncle spanked him with his hard, hard hoof.

He asked his broad aunt, the Hippopotamus, why her eyes were red and his broad aunt spanked him with her broad, broad hoof;

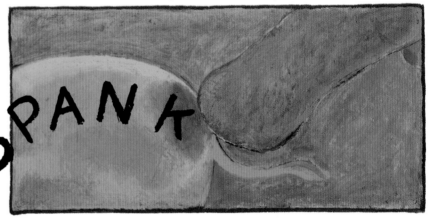

And he asked his hairy uncle, the Baboon, why melons tasted just so, and his hairy uncle spanked him with his hairy, hairy paw.

He asked questions about everything that he saw, or heard, or felt, or smelt, or touched, and all his uncles and his aunts spanked him. And still he was full of 'satiable curiosity!

One fine morning this Elephant's Child asked a new question that he had never asked before: "What does the Crocodile have for dinner?"

Everybody said, "Hush!" in a loud and dretful tone, and they spanked him for a long time.

BY AND BY, HE CAME UPON KOLOKOLO BIRD sitting in the middle of a wait-a-bit thorn-bush, and said, "My father has spanked me, and my mother has spanked me; all my aunts and uncles have spanked me for my 'satiable curiosity; and still I want to know what the Crocodile has for dinner!"

Then Kolokolo Bird said, with a mournful cry, "Go to the banks of the great grey-green, greasy Limpopo River and find out."

That very next morning this Elephant's Child took a hundred pounds of bananas (the little short, red kind),

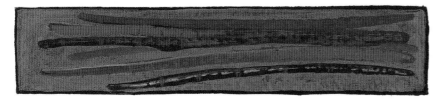

and a hundred pounds of sugar-cane (the long purple kind),

and seventeen melons (the greeny-crackly kind),

and said to all his dear families, "Goodbye. I am going to the great grey-green, greasy Limpopo River to find out what the Crocodile has for dinner."

THEN HE WENT AWAY, EATING MELONS and throwing the rind about, because he could not pick it up.

He went from Graham's Town to Kimberley, and from Kimberley to Khama's Country, and from Khama's Country he went east by north eating melons all the time, till at last he came to the banks of the great grey-green, greasy Limpopo River.

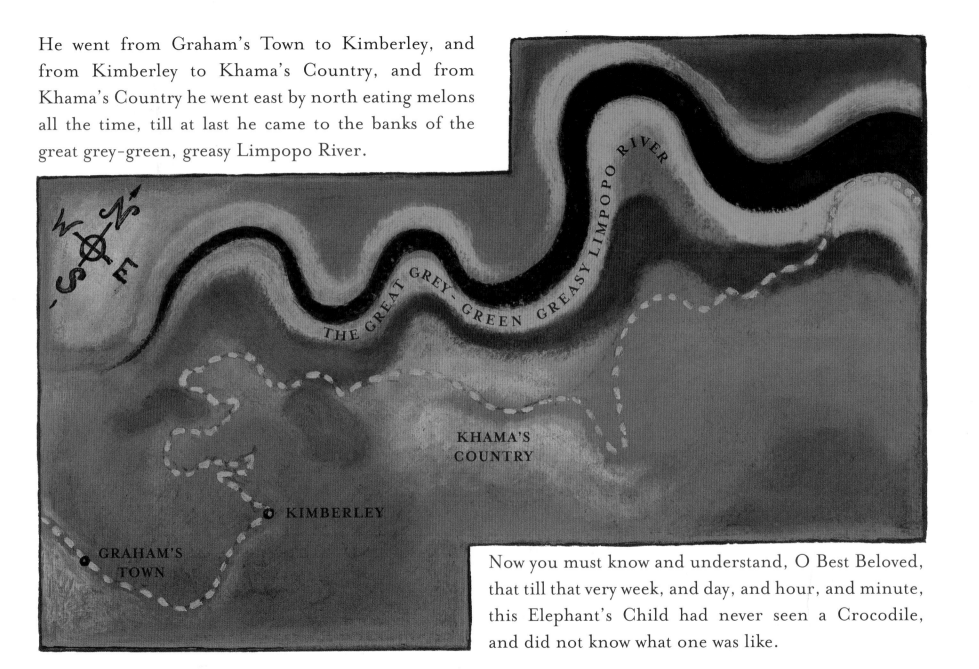

THE GREAT GREY-GREEN GREASY LIMPOPO RIVER

KHAMA'S COUNTRY

KIMBERLEY

GRAHAM'S TOWN

Now you must know and understand, O Best Beloved, that till that very week, and day, and hour, and minute, this Elephant's Child had never seen a Crocodile, and did not know what one was like.

THE FIRST THING THAT HE FOUND was a Bi-Coloured-Python-Rock-Snake curled round a rock.

"Scuse me," said the Elephant's Child politely, "but have you seen such a thing as a Crocodile in these promiscuous parts?"

"Have I seen a Crocodile?" said the Bi-Coloured-Python-Rock Snake, in a voice of dretful scorn. "What will you ask me next?"

"Scuse me," said the Elephant's Child, "but could you tell me what he has for dinner?" Then the Bi-Coloured-Python-Rock-Snake uncoiled himself very quickly and spanked the Elephant's Child with his scalesome, flailsome tail.

"That is odd," said the Elephant's Child, "because my father and my mother, and my uncle and my aunt, not to mention my other aunt and my other uncle, have all spanked me for my 'satiable curiosity."

HE SAID GOODBYE VERY POLITELY to the Bi-Coloured-Python-Rock-Snake, and helped to coil him up on the rock again, and went on eating melons, and throwing the rind about because he could not pick it up, till he trod on what he thought was a log of wood at the very edge of the great grey-green, greasy Limpopo River.

But it was really the Crocodile, O Best Beloved, and the Crocodile winked one eye.

Scuse me, but do you happen to have seen a crocodile in these parts?

"Scuse me," said the Elephant's Child most politely, "but do you happen to have seen a Crocodile in these promiscuous parts?"

Then the Crocodile winked the other eye, and lifted half his tail out of the mud; and the Elephant's Child stepped back most politely.

"COME HITHER, LITTLE ONE," said the Crocodile. "Why do you ask such things?"

"Scuse me," said the Elephant"s Child most politely, "but my father has spanked me, my mother has spanked me, not to mention my tall aunt and my tall uncle, who can kick ever so hard, as well as my broad aunt and my hairy uncle, and including the Bi-Coloured-Python-Rock-Snake with the scalesome, flailsome tail. I don't want to be spanked any more."

"Come hither, Little One," said the Crocodile, "for I am the Crocodile," and he wept crocodile-tears to show it was true.

Then the Elephant's Child kneeled down on the bank and said, "You are the very person I have been looking for all these long days. Will you please tell me what you have for dinner?"

"Come hither, Little One," said the Crocodile, "and I'll whisper."

Then the Elephant's Child put his head down close to the Crocodile's musky, tusky mouth, and the Crocodile caught him by his little nose.

"I think," said the Crocodile between his teeth, "today I will begin with Elephant's Child!"

At this, O Best Beloved, the Elephant's Child was much annoyed, and he said, speaking through his nose, "Led me go! You are hurtig be!"

Then the Bi-Coloured-Python-Rock-Snake scuffled down and said, "My young friend, if you do not now pull as hard as ever you can, it is my opinion that your acquaintance," (and by this he meant the Crocodile), "will jerk you into yonder limpid stream before you can say Jack Robinson."

Then the Elephant's Child sat back on his little haunches, and pulled, and pulled, and pulled, and his nose began to stretch. And the Crocodile floundered into the water and he **pulled**, and **pulled**, and **pulled**.

AND THE ELEPHANT'S CHILD'S NOSE kept on stretching; and the Elephant's Child spread all his little four legs and **pulled**, and **pulled**, and **pulled**, and his nose kept on stretching, and the Crocodile threshed his tail like an oar, and he **pulled**, and **pulled**, and **pulled**,

This is too buch for be!

and at each pull the Elephant's Child's nose grew longer and longer. Then the Elephant's Child felt his legs slipping, and he said through his nose, which was now nearly five feet long, **"This is too buch for be!"**

THEN THE BI-COLOURED-PYTHON-ROCK-SNAKE knotted himself in a double-clove-hitch round the Elephant's Child's hind legs, and said, "Rash and inexperienced traveller, we will now seriously devote ourselves to a little high tension, because if we do not, that yonder self-propelling man-of-war," (and by this, O Best Beloved, he meant the Crocodile), "will put an end to your future career."

So he **pulled**, and the Elephant's Child **pulled**, and the Crocodile **pulled**, but the Elephant's Child and the Bi-Coloured-Python-Rock-Snake **pulled** the hardest, and at last …

THE CROCODILE LET GO of the Elephant's Child's nose with a plop that you could hear up and down the Limpopo.

Then the Elephant's Child sat down hard; but he was careful to say "Thank you" to the Bi-Coloured-Python-Rock-Snake;

and he was kind to his poor nose, and wrapped it up in cool banana leaves, and hung it in the great grey-green, greasy Limpopo to cool.

"What are you doing that for?" said the Bi-Coloured-Python-Rock-Snake.

"Scuse me," said the Elephant's Child, "but my nose is badly out of shape, and I am waiting for it to shrink."

The Elephant's Child sat there for three days waiting for his nose to shrink. But it never grew any shorter. For, O Best Beloved, the Crocodile had pulled it out into a trunk the same as all Elephants have today.

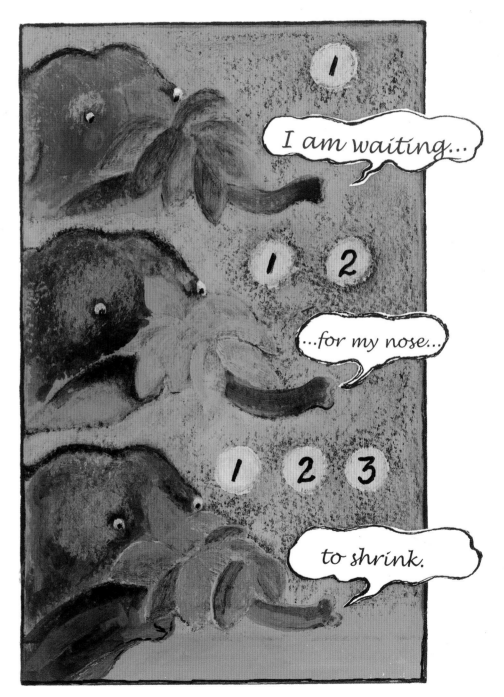

AT THE END OF THE THIRD DAY, a fly came and stung him on the shoulder. And before he knew what he was doing, he lifted up his trunk and hit that fly dead with the end of it.

"Vantage number one!" said the Bi-Coloured-Python-Rock-Snake. "You couldn't have done that with a mere-smear nose. Try and eat a little now."

"It is," said the Elephant's Child, and before he thought what he was doing he schlooped up a schloop of mud and slapped it on his head, where it made a cool schloopy-sloshy mud-cap all trickly behind his ears.

Vantage number two!

Vantage number three!

Before he thought what he was doing, the Elephant's Child put out his trunk, plucked a large bundle of grass and stuffed it into his mouth.

"Vantage number two!" said the Bi-Coloured-Python-Rock-Snake. You couldn't have done that with a mere-smear nose. Don't you think the sun is very hot here?"

"Vantage number three!" said the Bi-Coloured-Python-Rock-Snake. "You couldn't have done that with a mere-smear nose."

Now, HOW WOULD YOU LIKE to spank somebody?" said the Bi-Coloured-Python-Rock-Snake.

"I should like it very much indeed," said the Elephant's Child.

"Well," said the Bi-Coloured-Python-Rock-Snake, "you will find that new nose of yours very useful to spank people with."

"Thank you," said the Elephant's Child, "I'll remember that, and now I think I'll go home."

So the Elephant's Child went home across Africa, frisking and whisking his trunk. When he wanted fruit, he pulled fruit down from a tree. When he wanted grass, he plucked grass up from the ground. When the flies bit him, he broke off the branch of a tree and used it as a fly-whisk; and he made himself a new, cool, slushy-squshy mud-cap whenever the sun was hot. When he felt lonely, he sang to himself down his trunk, and the noise was louder than several brass bands.

He went especially out of his way to find a broad Hippopotamus (she was no relation of his), and he spanked her very hard, to make sure that the Bi-Coloured-Python-Rock-Snake had spoken the truth about his new trunk. And he picked up the melon rinds that he had dropped on his way to the Limpopo.

One dark evening he came back to all his dear families, and he coiled up his trunk and said, "How do you do?" They were very glad to see him, and said "Come here and be spanked for your 'satiable curiosity."

"Pooh," said the Elephant's Child. "I don't think you know anything about spanking. I'll show you."

Then he uncurled his trunk and knocked two of his dear brothers head over heels.

How do you do?

Where did you learn that trick?

I got it from a Crocodile!

"O Bananas!" said they. "Where did you learn that trick, and what have you done to your nose?"

"I got a new one from the Crocodile on the banks of the great grey-green, greasy Limpopo River," said the Elephant's Child.

"IT LOOKS VERY UGLY," said his uncle, the Baboon.

"It does," said the Elephant's Child. "But it's very useful." And he picked up his hairy uncle by one hairy leg, and hove him into a hornet's nest.

Then that bad Elephant's Child spanked all his dear families for a long time.

He pulled out his tall Ostrich aunt's tail-feathers; and he caught his tall uncle, the Giraffe, and dragged him through a thorn-bush, and he shouted at his aunt, the Hippopotamus, and blew bubbles into her ear when she was sleeping; but he never let anyone touch the Kolokolo Bird.

At last, things grew so exciting that his dear families went off one by one to the banks of the great grey-green, greasy Limpopo River to borrow new noses from the Crocodile.

When they came back, nobody spanked anybody any more; and ever since that day, O Best Beloved, all the elephants you will ever see have trunks like the trunk of the 'satiable Elephant's Child.